FREDDIE YETI

GOES TO SCHOOL

It was the first day of school and
Freddie Yeti was *NOT* ready.

Freddie did everything he could to avoid going to school.

He tried pretending he was sick.

He tried to pretend he lost his backpack.

He even tried to convince Mama Yeti that school was closed!

None of Freddie's plans worked.
Off to school he went.

Freddie didn't want to go to school because he didn't know what would happen there.

What if he got lost?

What if he couldn't make friends?

What if the teacher didn't like yetis?!

Mama Yeti told Freddie to be himself, try his best, and that everything would be okay.

Freddie was nervous as he stood outside the door about to enter his classroom for the very first time.

The bell rang and all the students entered the classroom. Freddie's first day of school had officially started.

Freddie put his backpack on a hook...

found his name tag at a table...

and sat down.

Freddie looked around. He looked a lot different than the other students.

Freddie was nervous no one would like him.

Freddie thought that maybe he should just try to blend in with his classmates. But then he remembered that he just needed to be himself, try his best, and then it would all be okay!

The day started with a good morning song,
which Freddie sang loud and proud.

Then, they moved on to math. Freddie liked counting, especially when candy was involved.

During art, Freddie discovered he could use a little
more practice with glue...

...but he was a master at coloring!

Freddie had a little trouble during writing. He mixed up some of his letters, but he kept practicing. He even earned a sticker for working so hard!

At recess, Freddie quickly learned that he was just the right height for dunking basketballs.

He even helped some friends reach the hoop!

At lunch, Freddie talked about his favorite dinosaurs with some of his classmates.

All throughout the day, Freddie followed Mama Yeti's advice. When something was hard, he tried his best and kept practicing!

"C..A..T.
C..Ca..Cat"

Instead of pretending to be like his classmates, Freddie was himself. Freddie even learned that he wasn't so different from the other students.

In fact, everyone in his class had their own differences that made them who they are!

fun with friends!

By the end of the day, Freddie had made lots of new friends...

and he had learned a lot!

alphabet project

When it was time to go home, Freddie was actually sad that he was leaving.

Even though the first day was scary at first, Freddie decided he liked school! When Mama Yeti came to pick him up, Freddie didn't want to leave!

Luckily, Mama Yeti told Freddie he could come back every day of the week! Freddie couldn't wait. School was his new favorite place.

Made in the USA
Coppell, TX
17 July 2020